The

Jan Dean writes p
short stories for ra

JAN DEAN

The Fight for Barrowby Hill

Illustrated by Jonathan Davies

PUFFIN BOOKS

For my mother and father

PUFFIN BOOKS

Published by the Penguin Group
Penguin Books Ltd, 27 Wrights Lane, London W8 5TZ, England
Penguin Books USA Inc., 375 Hudson Street, New York, New York 10014, USA
Penguin Books Australia Ltd, Ringwood, Victoria, Australia
Penguin Books Canada Ltd, 10 Alcorn Avenue, Toronto, Ontario, Canada M4V 3B2
Penguin Books (NZ) Ltd, 182–190 Wairau Road, Auckland 10, New Zealand

Penguin Books Ltd, Registered Offices: Harmondsworth, Middlesex, England

First published by Blackie Children's Books 1992
Published in Puffin Books 1994
10 9 8 7 6 5 4 3 2 1

Printed in England by Clays Ltd, St Ives plc
Filmset in Baskerville

Chapter One

'Order! Order!' The chairman of the meeting hammered the table, but no one took much notice.

Emma watched as her Aunt Caro and Uncle Richard stood at the front of a large group of protesters waving placards that said, 'Hands Off Barrowby!'

'If that was us up there,' cousin James said to Emma, 'we'd be in dead trouble.'

Emma knew what James meant. Grown-ups were always telling you to behave, weren't they?

'If we were shouting or waving our arms about like that we'd be marched straight out of class and straight into the headteacher's office. But when they do it it's a different story. They bend the rules when it suits them.'

All of this was true. Still, Emma felt a tremendous sympathy with the protesters. 'But Barrowby's a lovely place, James. Why should these Cruxton Housing people be allowed to come and build a new estate slap in the middle of it?'

'Ladies and gentlemen!' the chairman shouted again. 'If you do not resume your seats, I shall close the meeting.'

The hubbub calmed, but did not stop.

'This is my last warning,' he went on, red-faced with shouting, 'sit down or this meeting is over!'

Finally, the protesters settled down and Aunt Caro and Uncle Richard joined Emma and

James in their seats half-way down the hall.

'Help me with this, James,' Aunt Caro said, and together they slid her placard under their seats.

The chairman began his speech. The villagers had been invited to hear the facts about the proposed development in Barrowby. Too many rumours had been spread, too much gossip. It was time to set the record straight. The chairman was not a Barrowby man. He had come from the council office in Tonbridge and now he pinned maps and plans up on a board.

'Where are the new houses going to be?' Emma whispered to James.

'They haven't decided. That's why he's got all those maps.'

As soon as the man from the council had finished, a tall woman a few rows behind them was on her feet. 'I protest, Mr Chairman! None of these sites is suitable for development. I really think that the council should make that quite clear to these builders.'

'Who's that?' Emma wanted to know.

'Miss Bullen,' James groaned. 'She's our new teacher.'

'Don't you like her?'

'She's all right, I suppose. Only she's always on at me about healthy eating. She thinks I should lose weight.'

Emma said nothing. James did bulge rather. And he did eat quite a lot of sweets. Maybe Miss Bullen had a point.

'Cruxton Housing should take its plans and go elsewhere,' Miss Bullen was saying. 'Barrowby doesn't want them!'

'And who are you to say what Barrowby wants?' a gruff-voiced man from the front of the hall wanted to know.

'Yes, who put you in charge?' A discontented murmur rose in the hall.

'Oh, dear,' Aunt Caro said to Uncle Richard. 'I do hope Jenny Bullen doesn't turn the meeting against the protesters. She's fairly new to the village, just like us. It wouldn't do to make it seem that it's only us incomers who are against the builders. If she carries on laying the law down like that it will really put people's backs up.'

Not everyone in the village hall was against the plan. The vicar wanted to know what sort of houses Cruxton wanted to build. Would they be very expensive? He didn't think that luxury houses were a good idea.

'We need cheap houses in the village,' he said. 'It's wrong that young people have to move away because they can't afford to buy a home in the village they were born in.'

'That's right. Houses for locals, that's what we want!'

'Nobody is against that,' Aunt Caro said loudly and clearly. 'But these developers must choose their building land carefully. They mustn't be allowed to do just as they like.'

'Exactly,' Miss Bullen cried, on her feet once more. 'These people think they can walk all over us –'

'Shut up, Missus, or it's you who will get walked on.' The gruff-voiced man from the front stood up and turned to face Miss Bullen.

'Well, really.' Miss Bullen was offended. 'I won't be spoken to like that. Apologize at once or –'

'Or what? You going to keep me in after school?' The man grinned nastily and looked

around the hall. One or two people laughed.
'You're all mouth. You can't do nothing.'

'Who's that?' Emma asked.

'Alistair Drew,' James muttered. 'He has a
farm just outside the village.'

'I'll tell you what we can do, Mr Drew.' Miss
Bullen looked taller and thinner when she was
angry. 'We can form an Action Committee and
fight the developers.'

'Committee,' Drew sneered. 'Oh, that'll
really scare 'em. A lot of old ditherers writing
letters. Let Cruxton build their houses where
they like. So long as they pay for the land

that's their business. Meetings,' Alistair Drew laughed. 'Waste of time. Enough hot air to float a balloon. And in the end what can you do? Nothing.' And with that he walked out of the hall.

'Well!' Aunt Caro said as the meeting settled down again. 'Thank goodness all farmers aren't like him.'

'Don't think too badly of him,' Uncle Richard said quietly. 'The word in the village is that the Drews have hit hard times. They owe money all over the place. Selling a bit of land would solve a lot of problems for them.'

'Owning land doesn't mean you can do what you like with it,' Aunt Caro said stiffly.

Uncle Richard shook his head, 'I don't think Alistair Drew would agree with you there.'

'He doesn't care about Barrowby at all,' Emma said. 'He's horrible.'

Chapter Two

The next day Emma and James walked into Old Barrowby.

'You're so lucky to live here, James,' Emma said. 'I think Barrowby's a great place.'

'It's all right,' James said. 'There's not as much to do as in the town, though. It's OK for you just coming on holiday. You don't have time to get bored with it.'

'Bored! But it's such an exciting place. There's the woods and the hill, and all that swampy sort of place we got the tadpoles from at Easter.'

'Yeah, well, like I said, it's all right. Oh no!' James's face fell as he saw Miss Bullen walking towards them. 'Not her. Quick, let's go in here.' And he dragged Emma into the Post Office Stores.

'Right then, young James, what'll it be?' Mrs Godolphin's cheerful pink face smiled at them from behind the counter. 'Is it Post Office you're wanting, or Stores?'

James hesitated. 'Er, I'm not sure.' He hadn't planned a visit to the Stores. 'Emma,' he whispered, nudging her discreetly. 'I haven't got any money with me. Have you?'

'Honestly, James,' Emma grinned. 'What a complicated way of getting a Mars bar.'

'But I didn't plan it,' James protested. 'It's just that I didn't want to talk to –'

Before he had finished speaking Miss Bullen walked into the Stores, exactly as Mrs Godolphin handed the Mars bar to James.

'Thank you, dear. Enjoy your holiday,' she said as Emma paid her.

'Really, James,' Miss Bullen shook her head. 'You'll never improve your football if you don't improve your fitness.'

'I hate all that health stuff,' James moaned as he and Emma walked on through Barrowby. 'I really, really hate it.'

'Oh, I don't know,' Emma said. 'After all, James, you are a bit –'

'A bit what?' James turned angrily on Emma.

'Even Aunt Caro says you shouldn't eat so many –'

But James was not going to let her finish. 'You're not my mum and you're not my teacher, so don't tell me what to do.'

'I was only –'

'Sticking your nose in,' said James. 'Where it's not wanted.'

'I was thinking,' Emma said coolly, 'of climbing Barrowby Hill. But as you aren't interested in getting fit, I don't suppose you'll want to come with me.'

'No,' James almost shouted. 'I don't.'

He watched her as she walked the length of the village street and saw her turn up Wood Lane, towards the hill. All that fuss about a bit of chocolate, he thought, as he threw the wrapper in the bin. He was sorry now that he wasn't going with her.

Emma climbed the steep woodland path and came out at the top of Barrowby Hill. The sun was very hot and the grass smelt sweet and herby. She passed the old church that sat on the hilltop like a tall hat, then wandered into Church Meadow.

Way above her flew a small plane. It seemed no bigger than one of the bees that zigzagged over the field. Emma looked up at it. Why was it flying over Barrowby? Was it to do with the new houses? As Emma watched and wondered, the small plane began to circle almost directly overhead. The noise of the engine was so loud it hurt her ears. Suddenly it dipped low, buzzing angrily just a few feet above her head. It cast a dark shadow on the hill and Emma was inside the darkness. She felt afraid and suddenly angry. What right had it to come and spread its

cold wings over the summer hill? She began to run, but the plane moved with her. It seemed as if she would never break out of its shadow. Even the grass inside the darkness felt different. Hard and spiky like frozen grass. The hill hates the plane as much as I do, she thought. The ground under her feet seemed to prickle with anger. The plane grew louder again as it swooped above her. It was aiming for her, she was sure of it, trying to push her off the hill. Its engine snarled as it passed back and forth above her. No matter where she ran it could easily follow. Except the wood, she thought. It can't find me there. As she made for the shelter of the wood, the plane was so low she could almost see the pilot's face. Quickly she ran for the trees.

The green light of the wood closed about her like a curtain. All around her the trees whispered. It's like someone dreaming, she thought. The branches are tossing and turning and talking in their sleep. But above the soft shushing of the trees was the buzz of the plane flying directly overhead. It doesn't want me here, she thought, it's trying to chase me away.

The plane was even lower now and as it growled above the hill, the noise in the trees grew – no longer a sigh, but a fierce hiss. The whole wood seemed to be roaring. Strange grey mist sprang up amongst the roots and branches. It made the old tree trunks look like giant teeth. The growl of the plane was all around now and its dreadful noise burst down through the sheltering leaves. And then the hill shook. She felt it quite clearly. There was no mistake. The ground under her feet shuddered so that she stumbled and fell.

By now the mist was thick. So thick that Emma couldn't see the downhill track. Then something moved in the bushes below her. Oh,

James, Emma thought, I wish I hadn't fallen out with you. I wish you were here with me now. She heard the crack of a twig and the swish of a branch pushed aside. She stared towards the sound. Someone was coming towards her out of the mist.

Chapter Three

'Are you all right?' Matthew Waterwitch looked closely at Emma. Something had obviously frightened her and she seemed a little dazed. 'Did you bang your head?' he asked. 'The path is clearer lower down,' he smiled encouragingly. 'This is the only stretch where the trees make a tunnel.'

'No, I'm OK,' Emma said. 'It was the noise and all the mist.'

'That dreadful plane, you mean,' Matthew's face hardened. 'There's more than noise to worry about there. It's a crop-sprayer. It only has to be a few feet off-course to kill half the hedgerow.'

'It sounded so angry,' Emma went on. 'Then when the noises in the wood started and the mist . . .' She stopped when she saw his puzzled expression.

'Mist?' he asked. 'Do you mean that the plane has been spraying these woods?'

She shook her head. The mist that she had seen had risen from the ground beneath the woods, not fallen from above it.

'Well, there's no mist now,' Matthew said gently. 'I expect you did bang your head. Perhaps we'd better get you home. Where do you live? You're not from the village, are you?'

'No, I'm on holiday at my cousin's in New Barrowby.'

'Come on then,' Matthew said. 'You can show me where.'

'In the woods?' Aunt Caro was horrified. 'On your own?' She paused and stared hard at Emma. 'Thank you, Mr Waterwitch, for bringing her home. She can count herself lucky that she met you. Have you thought, Emma, that wandering around lonely places on your own isn't such a clever thing to do?'

Emma hung her head and mumbled some sort of answer. She hadn't meant to go off alone, it had just sort of happened.

But Aunt Caro was not going to let it go. Emma was in for a full-scale telling off. Matthew Waterwitch said his goodbyes and left.

'I don't know what James was thinking of, letting you go like that,' Aunt Caro said. 'Where is he now?'

'I don't know.'

'Wait till I see him,' Aunt Caro said and began to cut up sandwiches for tea. Emma felt guilty. If she hadn't nagged James about the Mars bar he would never have left her.

'It was my idea, Aunt Caro. I wanted to go by myself. It wasn't James's fault.'

'It's no use trying to cover up for him, Emma.'

'But –'

It was a losing battle. When James came in half an hour later Aunt Caro started on him.

'Well, young man, and what have you got to say for yourself?'

James looked sideways at Emma. What was this all about? Had she been telling tales?

'It's no use looking at Emma,' his mother said sharply, 'you're old enough to take responsibility for your actions, James. How could you leave her to go wandering about on her own like that? Anything could have happened. Anything!'

'I'm sorry, James, really I am.' Emma apologized after Aunt Caro had finished shouting. 'I told her it was my fault, but she wouldn't listen.'

'It's OK,' James shrugged. 'She gets like that when she's worried. Not happy until she's told off as many people as possible. Dad says that's why she'll be so good on Miss Bullen's Action Committee. As long as she's worried about Barrowby she'll never stop nagging the people who are threatening it.'

'Mmm,' said Emma, and James knew that she hadn't heard a word.

'What's wrong?'

'I'm not sure,' Emma said, 'but there was something very odd in the woods.' And she told him exactly what she'd seen and heard.

'And then it just disappeared?' James asked when she finished her story.

She nodded. 'Mr Waterwitch thought I'd bumped my head, but I did see mists, James, I *did*.'

'It was a hot day –'

'And I didn't have sunstroke either!' It was awful not to be believed.

'I was thinking that maybe you saw a heat haze,' James said and then Emma felt mean for having snapped at him.

'Well,' said James at last, 'I think that if you say you heard growling and saw mists, then you heard growling and saw mists. It would be stupid to make a thing like that up. There'd be no point in it. Come on.'

'Where are we going?' Emma asked.

'Back to the wood,' said James. 'Where else?'

'Tea!' Aunt Caro shouted from the kitchen. James hesitated.

'It's sandwiches,' Emma said. 'They'll keep.'

'Do you think we could take them with us? We might be out a long time.'

But Emma was giving him a look and one row about food was enough for one day, so he opened the front door and called back to his mother, 'We'll eat later. See you!' Then he and Emma set out.

Chapter Four

The road between the new village and Old Barrowby curved round the foot of Barrowby Hill. They were half-way along it when James turned off the road and into the narrow lane that was the short cut to Church Meadow. 'This way,' he said.

'Through the farm? Should we, James? Perhaps we'd better go through Old Barrowby.'

'This is much quicker.'

'I don't know,' Emma hesitated. 'Aren't we trespassing?'

'No, there's a footpath. The farmer's not very friendly and he tries to make you feel you've no right to be there, even though you have. But the farm's huge, so he probably won't see us. It'll be OK.'

'Meadowfield Farm,' Emma read the dilapidated sign that half hung from the gate. 'Could do with a lick of paint.' She thought for a moment, then she said, 'Church Meadow must

always have been important.'

'How do you mean?'

'Well, the whole farm is named after that one field. It's not called "Barleyfield Farm" or "Church Farm", is it?'

'No, it's not. I suppose you're right. The meadow must always have mattered. I wonder why?'

They were half-way up the farm track, between the barn and a tractor shed, when two men stepped out to meet them. Both of them were

frowning. Emma recognized the taller one at once. It was the gruff-voiced man who had been so nasty to Miss Bullen at the meeting.

'You might have told me that the unfriendly farmer was Alistair Drew,' Emma said. 'Who's the other one?'

'His brother Carl,' James whispered. 'Shall we go back?'

'If we're not trespassing and this really is a footpath,' Emma said, 'why should we? No, James, keep walking.'

'OK,' James sighed. 'Just our luck to run into the Drews.'

'Hey!' Carl Drew was staring hard at Emma. 'You again,' he growled. 'You're the one who was messing about on the hill. Nosying around. I saw you.'

Emma looked puzzled. She had been alone on the hill. How could he have seen her?

'You can see everything from where I sit,' he grinned. 'I sit real high up.'

'Mr Drew flies a crop-sprayer,' James explained. 'I expect his was the plane you saw this afternoon.'

'Another busybody,' Carl turned his

attention to James. 'Well, you're on Drew land now, so you can clear off. Go on. Do you hear me? Clear off.'

'We're on the public footpath, Mr Drew,' Emma said quietly. 'We won't stray from the path on to your land.'

'Public footpath,' sneered Carl Drew. 'Public nuisance, that's what you lot are. Poking around in places you're not wanted.'

'Cool down.' Alistair Drew laid a hand on his brother's arm and pulled him from the path. 'There'll be plenty of people coming this way soon if things go our way. You'll just have to get used to it.'

'Go on, then.' Carl's eyes were hard as steel. 'Walk along your public path.' And he made a mocking little bow as they passed him.

They felt his stare drill into their backs all the way across the farmyard.

'At least they let us through,' James said as they reached the other side. 'I thought they were going to throw us off the place.'

'They couldn't do that.' Emma closed the farm gate firmly behind her. 'Not if we were on a footpath.'

'You were really cool back there,' James said admiringly. 'I'll bet Miss Bullen could use you in her protest team.'

'Maybe I'll volunteer then.' Emma laughed. 'Race you to the top of the hill.'

Emma began to run up the steep slope. The faster she could leave the Drew brothers behind, the better.

'Come on, James,' she called. 'Get a move on.'

'Wait for me,' he complained, but she was at the top before he was half-way there.

While she waited for him she looked down the slope. Barrowby Hill rose above Meadowfield Farm like a huge green shoulder. The Drew brothers don't deserve this place, she thought.

'Oof!' James collapsed at her feet. 'Unfair. How am I supposed to race up hills on an empty stomach?'

Once he had got his breath back he and Emma walked towards the wood.

'What did Alistair Drew mean,' Emma asked, 'when he said plenty of people would be coming this way?'

'The new houses, of course,' James said. 'Cruxton Housing want to build on Church Meadow.'

'But they *can't*!' Emma could not believe it. They couldn't want to put houses on the hill. It was too beautiful. Too special. Surely anyone could see that?

'The Drew brothers,' James explained as they passed the church, 'are all in favour. There's a lot of money in it for them.'

'But they don't own the hill.'

'Of course they do, you chump,' James said. 'You said it yourself at the gate of Meadowfield Farm.'

'But . . .' Somehow there was no way of saying it. She only knew that James was wrong. The hill did not belong to the Drews. It belonged to itself. When Carl had tried to throw his cold shadow over the hill it had fought back. It would not give in to them.

From the corner of her eye, Emma saw something move. She looked round. A bush, heavy with elderberries, rustled. Emma looked hard at it, but could not see what was making its branches stir. Then below, near the roots, a yellow snake flashed briefly in the sun.

'James, look!' She pointed, but by the time he turned it had gone. 'Never mind,' she said and they went into the wood. He followed her to the place where she had seen the mist and heard the roaring. Birds sang. A squirrel ran up a thick trunk, then bounced from branch to branch above them.

'Well?' said James. Everything was perfectly normal.

'There was something here, I know it,' Emma said. 'I felt it.' Suddenly she lay down on the ground and pressed her ear close to the earth. 'Can you hear it, James?'

James crouched down beside her and listened too. Far underground there was a deep hissing

sound. It came and went, a bit like a bellows sucking and blowing. His eyes widened. 'Yes,' he whispered as if he only half believed it himself, 'I can.'

Chapter Five

The following morning Emma and James decided to go back to the hill.

'There are *other* places in Barrowby,' Aunt Caro said at breakfast. 'What about a picnic by the river?'

'Oh, leave them to it, Caro,' Uncle Richard said.

So Emma and James took their packed lunch and set off again for Church Meadow.

'Fancy the short cut?' James teased as they passed the farm track that led to Meadowfield.

'If you want,' Emma said. She didn't like the Drew brothers, but they were wrong to try and scare people off and Emma hated giving in when she felt she was in the right.

'I was joking, Em. I think we should steer clear. Anyway, we need to call in at the Stores, our picnic looks a bit small.'

So James and Emma took the long way round through the old village. They called at the Post Office Stores and James bought extra chocolate. Mrs Godolphin remembered Emma from her last visit.

'I thought you must be about,' she said as she gave them their change. 'Carl Drew was in here complaining about "interfering visitors staying in New Barrowby" and the only person I could think of to fit his description was you.' Emma blushed. Did Mrs Godolphin think she was an 'interfering visitor' too?

'Don't let him bother you, my dear,' she said. 'Them Drews were always bullies, like their father and grandfather before them. Nothing but bullies.'

'I won't, Mrs Godolphin,' said Emma. 'Thanks.'

They reached the small wooden sign which said 'To Barrowby Church' and followed its pointing arrow up Wood Lane. Ahead, the lane became a leafy uphill tunnel. They passed a row of three terraced cottages and James nodded to the end one. 'That's where your rescuer lives.'

'Mr Waterwitch?'

'Yes. The snake-man.'

'What?' Snake-man – what a creepy name. Emma was glad that she hadn't known that when she'd met him in the wood.

'Don't look so worried,' James laughed at her. 'He's interested in adders, that's all. He runs a wildlife hospital; his back garden's full of pens and cages.'

'How come he knows so much about animals?'

'He ought to,' said James. 'He's a vet.'

'I saw a snake on the hill yesterday. I don't think it was an adder, though.'

'A grass snake then. An olive-brown sort of colour?'

'No, yellow . . . well, gold really. It was very glittery.'

'I don't know what that is,' James said. 'Are you sure about the colour?'

'It was really bright. Like sun on a mirror.'

James was frowning. 'It can't have been.'

Emma hesitated. She remembered it so clearly – a flash of yellow moving through the grass like light. But then, she had only seen it for a second and she had turned her head very quickly. Maybe she'd been mistaken, dazzled for a moment.

'I'll ask Mr Waterwitch,' she said. 'Perhaps he'll have some pictures.'

The higher up the wooded slope they climbed, the more quiet they became.

'Ssh,' whispered Emma as they came to the place where they had heard the strange sounds in the earth.

'What was it, do you think?' she asked.

'Water?' he suggested. 'You heard a sort of roaring before and you saw mist. Maybe there are underground streams or something. Mist could rise from that.' James thought about it. 'Only . . .'

'What?'

'If the water was rising through the soil, I think the earth would be sort of marshy.'

He was right, of course. But the floor of the wood was dry, even dusty.

'Weird,' said Emma. 'I wonder if it's still there.'

They lay again and listened. There it was again.

'It's like breathing,' Emma said. 'Are there caves in the hill? It sort of echoes, like air moving in a huge cave.'

'I don't think there are caves,' James said uncertainly. 'We'll ask Dad when we get back. Come on, there's nothing else we can do here. Let's go to the churchyard.'

At the edge of the woods the air grew uncomfortably warm. The sun was a white fire in the sky; the open hilltop was an oven.

'Shall we go inside the church?' James asked. 'It's baking out here.' And Emma nodded in relief.

Chapter Six

The church porch was shady and the old studded door creaked slightly as they went in. It was very quiet inside and wonderfully cool. Emma took a deep breath. The air smelled of beeswax polish and flowers. It was lovely.

'It's a very old church,' said James. 'Dad says the walls would have been covered in bright-coloured paintings once.'

'Really?' Emma couldn't imagine it. The plain white-washed walls seemed so right somehow.

'The carvings are great,' James said. 'Look at this one.' James pointed to a panel showing a roly-poly farmer being pitchforked by a laughing devil. 'It's a warning,' he went on. 'It means: Be careful that money doesn't end up sending you to hell.'

'Really?' Emma asked. 'How can you tell all that from one little picture?'

'They're a sort of code,' James explained.

'When these were carved hardly anybody could read, so they used pictures. The fat farmer is a rich farmer. You only got to be fat if you could afford to eat well, so fat means rich.'

'I see,' Emma smiled as she prodded James's round stomach. 'Look out for devils with pitchforks then, James.'

'Watch it,' he said, but she could see that he hadn't minded her teasing.

'Where have the carvings come from?' Emma asked. 'They weren't here before.'

'They were,' James said, 'but covered up. They were underneath the plain oak panels and when the restorers came to do repairs they found these underneath. This is my favourite.'

It was a dragon. It filled the whole panel. In the foreground there was a knight.

'St George?'

'I don't think so,' said James. 'It doesn't look as if they're fighting. The knight's sword is stuck in the ground.'

'Is it a sword?'

It wasn't. It was a staff, carved like twisted snakes.

'That's to do with doctors isn't it, that snake-

stick thing? I'm sure I've seen something like it in the chemist's.' Emma stared at the carving.

'He doesn't look like a doctor, but he doesn't look like a warrior either,' James said thoughtfully. 'Strange, isn't it?'

'He's a shepherd,' Emma said suddenly. 'That's not a staff, it's a shepherd's crook.' And anyway, she thought, he's obviously a man who looks after things, he's got that sort of face.

'If he's a shepherd,' James cocked his head to one side and studied the carving, 'then where's his dog? He'd have needed a dog to scare off sheep-stealers and wolves, wouldn't he?'

'Ah,' Emma laughed. 'He's gone one better than that. He's got a dragon.'

'Look out wolves, then,' James grinned, and ran his fingers along its carved scaly coils.

'Are there any more carvings?' Emma asked.

'There's one over there.' James nodded across the aisle and they went to look at it. It was a picture of a feast.

'Come on,' said James. 'Looking at this is making me hungry. Let's have our picnic in Church Meadow.'

Outside they heard voices. It was Matthew Waterwitch and the vicar. They were crouched down by the churchyard gate.

'That's the third today,' Matthew said.

'And there were the field mice,' the vicar sighed.

When James and Emma reached them they saw the two men examining a dead hedgehog.

'There are flowers dying too,' Matthew said. 'All over the hill things are dying.'

'Ah!' Emma cried out as if she had been stung or bitten.

'What's the matter? Are you all right?'

Matthew's voice was soft and concerned.

'I think it was an electric shock.' Emma felt dazed.

'A shock?' Matthew glanced around for anything that might have caused it.

'The ground sort of *prickled*. Like static.' Emma tried to explain it. 'Didn't you feel it?'

But nobody else had felt anything at all. Emma began to feel awkward.

'The sun is awfully fierce today,' the vicar said. 'Have you a headache?'

'I'm fine, thank you,' Emma said. 'Come on, James, let's have our lunch.'

'It was *not* my imagination,' she said as she and James sat down to eat.

'I never said it was.'

'Do you think it's got anything to do with the noises underground?' she asked.

But before James had a chance to reply, Matthew Waterwitch walked down the slope and joined them.

'They won't really build houses here, will they?' Emma asked him.

'I hope not,' said Matthew. 'Though they will if the Drews get their way.'

'Can't they see how beautiful it is?'

Matthew laughed. 'I don't think beauty cuts much ice with the Drews,' he said at last. 'They wanted to plough it up and grow barley, but the deeds of the farm don't allow it. It's for grazing. It was common land once, but Meadowfield Farm swallowed it up generations ago. Still, it can't be ploughed and cropped. The deeds are quite clear on that. Now the Drews are trying to sell it to Cruxton Housing, but we're fighting it.'

'But if the deeds won't let them plough it for farming – ?'

'I'm afraid the Drews have found a legal loophole. If they want to sell it to Cruxton Housing, they can. Cruxton won't be "ploughing and cropping", you see. And whoever put that clause in the deeds all those years ago never imagined houses on the hill, so . . .'

'It doesn't seem fair,' said James.

'No,' said Matthew. 'It doesn't. This hill has been undisturbed for hundreds and hundreds of years. Those trees back there are the wild-wood – the last remains of the great forests that once covered the whole of Britain. And this

47

meadow is really special. Rare plants grow here. Butterflies that are dying out in other places still live here. We're trying to have it made into an SSSI. If we succeed, that'll put a stop to Carl and Alistair Drew's plans once and for all.'

'An SSSI?'

'Site of Special Scientific Interest. The inspector will be here in a few days' time.'

'So the hill will be safe?'

'Mmmm.' Matthew's eyes clouded. 'If he comes in time.'

'What do you mean?'

'Something's poisoning the earth. Things are dying. If he doesn't come soon it'll be too late.'

'Poor old Barrowby Hill.' Emma rolled over on the grass and stroked it.

'*Worm Hill*, you mean,' Matthew said. 'Barrowby Hill is just the name for maps and tourists. Its old name is Worm Hill. It's mentioned in the *Domesday Book*.'

'Must be a fairly big worm,' James said with a grin, 'to make a hill this size.'

Matthew laughed. 'It probably means "snake",' he explained. 'There are lots of adders round here and at one time "worm" meant "snake" and even "dragon".'

'There's a dragon in the church,' Emma said. 'And a man with a snake-stick.'

'The dragon *is* the hill,' Matthew said. 'That's why it fills the picture. A dragon looking like a hill is a way of telling us the name of the hill. Clever, isn't it?'

And so simple and straightforward. Emma felt strangely disappointed.

Chapter Seven

Back home Aunt Caro had a job for them. Miss Bullen's Action Committee had had posters and leaflets printed explaining exactly why Cruxton Housing should not build their new estate on Church Meadow. Aunt Caro was helping to spread the word.

'Right,' she said. 'These are to go to every house in the village. No exceptions. No cutting corners. OK?'

'OK,' they said, and armed with leaflets marked 'Save Barrowby Hill', James and Emma set off to deliver them.

'Some of these letter-boxes are a bit fierce,' Emma complained as they went round New Barrowby.

'Leave them on the doorstep then,' James suggested. But Emma didn't. The leaflets were only light. They might blow away.

Once they had finished in New Barrowby, they set off for the old village. Half-way along the road was the entrance to Meadowfield Farm.

'You must be kidding,' James said as Emma turned up the path. 'The Drews want to sell Church Meadow, not save it.'

But Emma's jaw was set in a hard line. '*Every* house, Aunt Caro said. Come on.'

The hill rose above Meadowfield Farm like a green wave. A wind came from nowhere and stirred the grass. It rippled on the meadow like the scales of a fish.

'It looks alive, doesn't it?' said James.

Suddenly, the wind from the hill gusted. The farmhouse windows rattled, two empty flower-pots fell and rolled on the concrete path. The barn door swung back and banged and banged behind them. They turned to look. Inside the barn, a large black tarpaulin flapped. Under-neath it, a stack of chemical drums squatted like an evil yellow pyramid.

'You!' Carl Drew appeared out of the barn, his arm raised threateningly. 'Get out of here, you.' His eyes were little angry slits, his words came from between clenched teeth. 'Nosy inter-fering incomers. What do you know about Barrowby? Your houses are built on old

farmland, but you don't want any more in case they spoil your pretty village! Hypocrites, that's what you are.' He towered above them. 'And you can give that rubbish to me.'

Before they could stop him, Carl Drew snatched the remaining leaflets from their hands and tore them into shreds. 'Waste paper, that's all it is. Worth nothing.'

The seething wind lifted the scraps of paper and spun them round him like a snowstorm. It knows what they're doing, Emma thought. The hill knows that they are its enemies. Above the wood, the sky darkened and lightning forked in the angry sky.

'Get off my land.' Carl Drew's voice was low and menacing. He stepped towards them, so close that Emma could smell his sweat and the petrolly scent of machines. 'If I catch you here again you'll know all about trouble,' he said. 'Go on.' He raised his fist. 'Out!'

And James and Emma turned and ran from the yard.

They stopped outside the farm gate. James was breathless. 'What now?' he gasped. 'Back home?'

But Emma was angry. 'No,' she said. 'We have leaflets to deliver.'

'How can we when Drew tore them up?'

'We'll just have to get some more, then. Aunt Caro got the last lot from Mr Godolphin. Come on.' With that, she set off for Old Barrowby.

'Wait for me,' James wheezed as he tried to keep up with her.

'Goodness, you look quite pale,' Mrs Godolphin said as Emma went into the Post Office Stores.

'It was Mr Drew,' Emma said. 'I thought he was going to hit us.'

'He tore up our leaflets,' James added and then told her the whole story.

'Them Drews.' Mrs Godolphin pursed her lips in disapproval. 'We all know things are bad for them right now, but they've no call to go taking it out on you.'

'The thing is, Mrs Godolphin, have you got any more?'

'A boxful, in the back,' she smiled.

'Could we have some, do you think?' James went on. 'Mum wanted us to do all of the village, you see.'

'Course you can, my dears.' She bustled into the back of the shop and came back with a small cardboard box. 'They're really for Mr Waterwitch to take into Tonbridge. He's going to put some in the library and let the Conservation Society have a few. Still, I don't suppose he'll mind you having some.'

'It isn't just the newcomers who want to save the hill, is it, Mrs Godolphin? Mr Drew said it was. He said we were interfering outsiders.'

'The nerve! Godolphin's very keen on this protest thing. He says they've no right to build on the hill. And them Drews 've no business calling other folks outsiders. Why that Drew family haven't been in Barrowby five minutes. Old Man Drew – that's Carl and Alistair's grandfather – only got that land in the war. He bullied Hester Waterwitch. Browbeat her. Her son was missing in action, you see. She thought there'd be no more Waterwitches to farm the land. And what with Old Man Drew going on and on . . . well, in the end she just gave in.'

'And Hester Waterwitch was – ?'

'The present Mr Waterwitch's grandmother. His father came home from the war to find the family farm was sold. He never really got over it. They tried to buy it back, but them Drews . . . downright nasty they are. Not Barrowby people at all. Oh no, that family comes from some run-down hole the other side of the Downs.'

Emma and James said goodbye and walked round old Barrowby delivering the rest of the leaflets. Emma was feeling better. The shock of Carl Drew's anger had left her shaky, but Mrs Godolphin's kindness was a good cure.

'"Five minutes," Mrs Godolphin said the Drews had been in Barrowby,' Emma murmured and grinned, 'and she meant fifty years. Not much hope for the people of New Barrowby, is there?'

Chapter Eight

At the corner of Wood Lane they saw Matthew in his garden. When he saw their leaflets, he smiled and asked them in for tea.

'It's only shop cake, I'm afraid,' Matthew said. 'I'm not much of a cook.'

'Swiss roll's my favourite,' James mumbled, his mouth half-full. 'We call it "snail cake" at home.'

'Snail?' Matthew pulled a face. 'Why ever – oh, I see, the way the jam winds through the sponge. I suppose it is a bit like a snail shell. Doesn't the idea put you off eating it, though?'

'Put James off eating?' Emma grinned. 'That's a laugh.'

'Mmm,' Matthew agreed as they watched James help himself to his third slice.

'Want to look round?' Matthew asked them when they'd finished. 'I've some wild rabbits in a pen at the back and a fox with its leg in splints in the shed.'

Matthew let them hold the young rabbits. Through their soft fur their hearts were beating very fast.

'Is its heart racing like that because it's scared?' James asked. 'Is it scared of us?'

'No, they're quite used to being handled now. Their hearts beat quite fast anyway. Small animals are like that.'

'Will you keep them?'

Matthew shook his head. 'They'll be back in the wild as soon as they're fit enough. Look.' Gently he lifted Emma's rabbit and stroked back the fur of its leg. A patch of bare skin was healing nicely. 'A woman in the village brought these in. She'd found some lads setting a dog on them.'

'How cruel!'

'I'll never understand it,' Matthew sighed, 'but some people are never happy unless they're picking on things weaker than themselves. Like to see the fox?'

'Phew!' James held his nose as they went into the shed.

Matthew laughed. 'How long have you lived in Barrowby, James?'

'About three years,' James said.

'And still not used to the fact that the countryside doesn't always smell as good as it looks?' Matthew teased. 'You do have a point, I will admit,' and he laughed again. 'A fox can smell pretty strong.'

'Oh, James,' Emma whispered, 'isn't he lovely?' The red pointy ears and the bright green eyes pricked with interest at their approach. 'What happened to him?'

'A car. Sometimes wild creatures just freeze in headlights, which isn't the best thing to do

if a car is coming straight at you.'

'Poor thing,' Emma said. 'Will his leg be all right?'

'Probably. I expect he'll be back in the woods again before long.'

'Better teach him the green cross code before you let him go,' James said.

'That,' said Matthew Waterwitch, 'is not a bad idea.'

'Do you like being a vet?' Emma wanted to know.

'Yes, I do. I've never wanted to do anything else.'

'Not farming?' James asked. 'Mrs Godolphin told us that Meadowfield Farm used to belong to your family.'

'Yes, it did. The Waterwitches farmed in Barrowby for hundreds of years.'

'You wouldn't sell Church Meadow to Cruxton Housing, would you?' Matthew shook his head.

'Well, of course he wouldn't,' Emma said angrily. 'That's a silly idea, James. Does it ever make you sad that your family don't live there any more?'

'It made my father sad. He'd have liked to farm, you see. When he came home from the war and found that my grandmother had sold the place he was furious. He left the village. He never came back here. He said seeing the Drews in Meadowfield would break his heart. He died in the town.'

'But you came back,' Emma said.

'My grandmother left me this cottage. It's where she moved to after she'd sold the farm. I've always been happy here.'

'Do you hate the Drews too, like your father did?' Emma asked quietly.

'I don't hate anybody,' Matthew answered. 'I just wish Church Meadow belonged to someone who'd look after it.'

It was almost dusk when they left.

'You forgot to ask him about the snake you saw,' James reminded Emma.

'Mmm.' She did not want to talk about the snake. 'I decided not to,' she said. Matthew hadn't seen the mist or felt the electricity. He hadn't heard the roaring or the sounds coming from the hill. But he should have done. The Waterwitches had been the guardians of Church Meadow for generations until Matthew's grandmother had sold the land. Why was she the one and not Matthew?

The sputter of an engine cut across her thoughts. Carl Drew's plane flew low above them. Its shadow moved across the fields like a shark rising through the water. That's it, Emma thought, it was all to do with that first day when she'd been angry with Carl Drew and his plane. Somehow, the hill had understood that she was on its side.

'Drew's crop-sprayer,' James said disgustedly. 'Isn't he out a bit late – it's practically dark.'

'The chemicals!' Emma cried. 'In the Drews' barn. We never told Matthew.'

So James and Emma hurried back through old Barrowby to Matthew Waterwitch's house.

Chapter Nine

When James and Emma got back from Matthew's they were in trouble.

'You,' said Aunt Caro sternly, 'are late again.'

But when James told her about the incident at Meadowfield Farm she softened.

'Those dreadful men,' she said. 'I ought to go round there right now and give them a piece of my mind!'

'I shouldn't, dear,' Uncle Richard said. 'It wasn't very tactful, taking leaflets to the Drews' place, was it? No wonder they flew off the handle.'

'Perhaps you're right,' Aunt Caro agreed reluctantly. 'Still, they shouldn't have spoken to the children like that.'

'Dad,' asked James, 'are there any underground wells or caves in Barrowby Hill?'

'Caves? No, I don't think so.'

'It's not hollow, then?'

'Not as far as I know. Why?'

'Whatever are you up to now?' Aunt Caro cut in suspiciously. 'Caves are very dangerous places and neither you nor Emma are to go anywhere near them.'

Well, that won't be hard, thought James, seeing as there aren't any.

'No streams, no caves,' James said to Emma as they walked upstairs at bedtime. 'Still, vibrations can travel a long way through the earth. Maybe we were just hearing traffic on the road or something.'

'What road? The road's miles away,' Emma said. 'We should tell Matthew about it. You never know, it could turn out to be useful. Something that could stop Cruxton Housing building on the hill.'

The thought cheered Emma up and she went to bed planning what she'd say to Matthew the next time she saw him.

Next morning at breakfast, Uncle Richard was curious about the lightning they had seen over the hill. 'I met the vicar last night,' he said.

'He wanted to know exactly when you saw it.'

'When that awful man tore up our leaflets,' Emma said.

'It was over the wood,' said James.

'There's been some damage on the hill. I suppose lightning might explain it,' Uncle Richard went on. 'At least, some of it.'

'What sort of damage?'

'Some trees have been uprooted. And the churchyard wall is almost demolished in places. Two gravestones have fallen over. More like an earth tremor than a lightning strike really. Still, you never know.'

'Or vandalism,' James suggested. 'Maybe the Drews –'

'No,' said Emma. 'It wasn't them.' But she couldn't say why she felt so certain.

They set off for Matthew's house but were saved a journey. He was outside the Post Office, talking to Carl Drew.

'It's all above board,' Drew snapped. 'Our farm's safer than the airfield. It's *private*, see. No one comes messing around. That's why I keep those drums in my barn. There are all sorts of comings and goings down by the hangars. Any-

one could get at them there. And it's dangerous
stuff in them drums, see, so I keep it in my own
place where I can keep an eye on it. Not that it's
anything to do with you, Mr Nosy Parker
Waterwitch.'

James and Emma waited while Carl Drew
climbed into his Land-Rover and drove away,
then they went over to Matthew.

'It's no good, I'm afraid,' he said. 'Drew isn't
hiding those chemicals. It's all legal and above
board.'

'He's lying,' Emma said.

'I'm afraid we need proof of that, Emma.' Matthew shook his head sadly.

'But it's obvious,' she almost shouted. 'It must be them. Who else would do it? The Drews are poisoning Church Meadow, killing all the special things that live there. Then when the Inspector comes, there'll be no reason to make it an SSSI. And if it's not an SSSI, then the Drews will sell to Cruxton Housing and they'll build an estate all over the hill.'

'Emma, Emma,' Matthew tried to calm her down. 'I'm sure you're right, but we really do have to have solid evidence. And I have to be very careful – Carl Drew's already saying that I'm spreading lies about them. If people start to believe him then they may not believe me if we do find proof.'

'But why should you tell lies about them?'

'He's saying I'm jealous.'

'Of the Drews?' James's voice rose in disbelief. 'Whatever for?'

'Because of Meadowfield Farm,' Emma said. She saw it at once. 'And plenty of people will believe him. If your dad hated the Drews it would seem only natural for you to hate them too.'

'And get back at them any way I can. Exactly.'

'But it's a lie!' James said indignantly.

'The Drews seem to be good at lies, don't they?'

It all seemed so hopeless that James and Emma hadn't the heart to do anything. They went home and spent the rest of the day moping around the house.

Chapter Ten

It was Saturday, so Uncle Richard went with James and Emma to see the damage on the hill. The vicar and Mr Godolphin were in the churchyard tidying up some of the disarray.

'I can't think what might have done it,' the vicar shook his head, as he piled the spilled stones of the wall back into some sort of order.

'Subsidence?' ventured Uncle Richard.

Mr Godolphin laughed. 'This church has stood a thousand years. It's not about to fall down now.'

While Uncle Richard talked to the vicar, James and Emma wandered through the churchyard.

'Not all of the damage is in here,' James pointed out. 'Those bushes over there are almost completely uprooted.'

Emma looked towards the bushes. 'That's where I saw the snake,' she said and remembered how it had moved over the grass like a ripple of bright electricity.

They went through the lich-gate for a closer look.

'James,' she said, as they drew nearer. 'There's something in the middle of those branches.'

Sure enough, in the centre of the matted twigs there was a greener ivy-covered mass.

'Quick, help me move these!'

James and Emma worked hard, pulling back the whippy elder twigs and dragging at the branches until the shape in the middle was exposed. It was a grey stone man holding some kind of rod.

'It's a statue,' James said, peeling off the clinging ivy.

'It's the man from the dragon-carving in the church,' Emma said. 'The man with the snake-stick.'

'Are you sure?' James asked. 'It's so worn and so covered with this creeping stuff – hey!' As he tore away the last of the ivy, the stone stick with its two stone snakes could be seen quite clearly.

Sssss . . .

Emma heard the hissing. Was the snake, the one she'd seen before, still there? She looked anxiously at the grass around her feet. There was nothing there, yet she could feel a dry warm coiling around her ankles. The hairs on the back of her neck rose.

Sssss . . .

She felt its grip and its releasing slither as it left her foot. She heard the rustle of the grass. And all the time she stared at the ground. There was nothing to be seen.

'James.' Her voice was hardly a whisper, but James wasn't even looking. He was gazing across to the churchyard where his father was waving angrily.

'James! James! Stop that at once!' Uncle Richard was shouting. 'Whatever are you doing to that tree?' But as soon as he was close enough to get a good look, he calmed down. The bushes were pulled right out of the ground – James and Emma could not possibly have done that.

'Look what we've found.'

'It's the man from the carving,' James explained.

'Good heavens,' said Mr Godolphin from the lich-gate. 'That's the Watchman!'

Uncle Richard, Mr Godolphin and the vicar pulled the uprooted elder bushes right away from the statue.

'I haven't seen him since I was a boy,' Mr Godolphin marvelled. 'I'd almost forgotten about him.'

'Who is it?' Uncle Richard asked.

'The Barrowby Watchman,' Mr Godolphin said. 'At least, that's what my mother used to call him.'

'And who exactly was he?'

'Bit of a local legend, really. He's supposed to take care of the land, come to our aid in time of trouble, that sort of thing. In the last war, German planes used to ditch their unused bombs over Sussex on their way home after they'd been blitzing London. Barrowby never got hit, though other villages round here did. There were some who said that was thanks to the Watchman. Some say it was the Watchman who saved us on the night a stray bomb exploded in the air above the hill. Others say it was a freak storm that did it. But who knows? Not a crumb of Barrowby soil was ever more than scratched by enemy shrapnel, I do know that.'

Emma ran her hand over the grey stone of the statue. 'He should be inside the hill,' she said.

'What a funny thing to say.' Uncle Richard looked at her oddly.

'It's all inside out,' she explained. 'Stone is from the middle of the earth, isn't it? With soil and grass on top. Yet here he is, a bit of the inside of the hill that's somehow got outside.'

'The heart of the hill, do you mean?' The vicar

seemed interested in the idea. 'Yes. I like that.'

'See them snakes.' Mr Godolphin pointed to the Watchman's staff. 'My grandma used to say if you stroked them snakes you'd be safe from adder bite.'

'Local lore, eh?' the vicar smiled. 'What a shame he's been left to get all overgrown like this.'

'Our last vicar wouldn't have agreed with you,' Mr Godolphin said. 'He wouldn't have folks using charms against adders. Nothing like that. He didn't like the Watchman at all. Mind you, I can understand that. The Watchman's been here a long time, maybe longer than the church. He's to do with superstition, not proper religion.'

'But he's part of Barrowby,' Uncle Richard protested. 'You can enjoy a local legend and preserve a landmark without believing in all the claptrap, can't you?'

'That's not how our last vicar saw it. He said the Watchman wasn't on church land and stopped the verger tidying up the ground round him.'

'Well,' the vicar said, 'I still think it's a

shame he's been neglected. Someone could have taken care of him. He's such an interesting sort of fellow.'

'Ah,' Mr Godolphin grunted. 'Strictly speaking, this bit of land back here is part of Church Meadow.'

'The Drews,' sighed the vicar.

'You wouldn't catch them looking after a statue, would you? Not unless there was money in it.'

'Well, we'll take care of him from now on,' said the vicar. 'He's a bit of Barrowby history and deserves better treatment than he's had at the hands of the Drews.'

'Yes,' Mr Godolphin said. Then he paused and looked slightly puzzled. 'Funny how your memory plays tricks, isn't it? I thought the old Watchman faced the other way. As I recall he stood with his back to the church and his face to the woods and the path down to the village. Now he's looking the other way.'

'Well,' said James, 'he's the Watchman, so he's watching the village.'

'Yes,' said Mr Godolphin, 'but that's New Barrowby. When I was a boy there was no

New Barrowby, so what was he watching then?'

'Strange about Mr Godolphin remembering the Watchman the wrong way round,' said James to Emma as they walked home.

'I don't think he did,' Emma said carefully so that Uncle Richard should not hear. 'I think the Watchman turned around. That's what caused the tremor on the hill.'

It was another hot night. The weather forecast had promised storms.

'It'll be a relief to have a thunderstorm,' Aunt Caro said. 'Clear the air.'

Neither James nor Emma went to sleep easily. Round about ten o'clock James called out and his father went in to see what was the matter.

'Dreaming, Caro,' he explained when he came down again. 'I expect it's the weather. Will it break tonight, do you think, like the forecast said?'

By midnight it was almost unbearably clammy. Emma woke uncomfortable, her nightdress sticking to her. She got out of bed and opened her window as wide as it would go. The moonlight was fuzzy and muffled by patchy cloud, but for a second it cleared and the white moon shone over the hill. Someone was moving out there, stealthily, in Church Meadow.

Chapter Eleven

Quietly, Emma crept into James's room and woke him.

'We can get the evidence,' she whispered. 'If we get close and we see exactly what they're doing, we'll have proof. Then we've won.'

Groggy with sleep, James climbed out of bed.

'Ssh,' Emma held a finger to her lips. 'If your mum hears us we've had it.'

Five minutes later, Emma and James left by the back door. They made their way along the road until they came to the lane which led to the hill – the short cut which went through Meadowfield Farm.

'This way?' James asked uncertainly.

Emma nodded. It would take too long through the woods, and the path would be tricky in the dark.

Their breathing sounded very loud in the quiet of the night. So loud that when they passed through the farmyard and reached the foot of the hill, they tried to breathe in whispers.

'I can't see anyone,' James murmured. 'Are you sure there was – ?' But then they heard voices. The Drew brothers were not on the hill at all, but in the yard somewhere, behind them.

'They must have come back for more stuff,' Emma whispered urgently. 'We need a place where we can hide and watch. Make for the churchyard. Quick, before they come.' And keeping in the shadow of the hedge, she sprinted up the slope like a hare.

James followed as best he could, running

hard till his heart banged in his chest and every snatched breath hurt. Finally, he caught up with her, and taking shelter by the churchyard wall he crouched down, panting desperately. He was only just in time, for as he dropped to the ground the Drew brothers came out of the farmyard and on to the hill.

'Be quiet, James!' Emma hissed. 'You sound like a train. They'll hear us.' And poor James did his best to breathe less noisily. They watched as the Drews, each carrying a flat square can, moved across the slope. They splashed pesticide about them as they came, slopping it over the rare and beautiful plants.

'There's your proof,' James whispered.

'We can't just watch,' Emma said. 'We've got to stop them. They're killing the hill.' And with that, she sped down the meadow, making straight for the Drews.

'What the – ?' Carl Drew stopped, startled.

'This is evidence,' Emma cried out, grabbing Carl's can and holding it high in the air. 'You've been poisoning the hill and we've caught you.' She turned to run back up the hill, but Carl Drew was too fast for her. Before she could get away he had her by the shoulder.

'Why so you have,' he grinned. 'Quite the little detective. Pity you won't be able to do anything about it.' Carl's eyes narrowed as he stared at Emma. 'A kid like you should be in bed,' he said. 'You could catch your death wandering the hill at night.'

Overhead the first thunder rumbled. The forecast storm was on its way.

'Farms are dangerous places to play about in. Especially in the dark,' he went on, twisting Emma's arm painfully behind her. 'Your mum

and dad should have told you that.'

The wind was gusting now. It had come from nowhere, but all the tree-tops of the wildwoods were whipping madly in the air. More thunder growled.

'Carl –' Alistair sounded anxious. 'What are you talking about?'

'We can't let her go now,' Carl said. 'She's seen everything. We'll be ruined if this gets out.'

'But –'

'But nothing. You always were too soft. There's a lot of money at stake here, not just a few quid. And this is our last chance. I warned her not to go sticking her nose in where it wasn't wanted. She should have listened.' Carl's voice was low, but bright and hard as a needle. Emma shivered when she saw the desperate gleam in his eyes. 'I reckon she'll have a nasty fall in our barn,' he said. 'Kids have suffocated in hay before now.'

The thunder was amazingly loud now. The whole hill boomed with it like a drum.

'We'd best head for shelter,' Alistair said. 'We'll talk about this there.' He turned away from his brother and as he did so, from the corner of his eye he caught a movement from the hill.

'Hang on, Carl.' Alistair Drew reached out and touched his brother's arm. 'There's another of them over there; it'll be that fat boy.' And he set off up the hill in James's direction.

Emma kicked and screamed, but it was no use. Carl Drew hauled her up the hill with him while his brother Alistair ran on ahead.

'He's in the churchyard!' shouted Carl, and Alistair vaulted easily over the wall. James zigzagged between the gravestones, trying to dodge Alistair, but every move seemed to narrow the gap between them.

'Run for the woods, James!' Emma screamed. 'Hide!' Then she bent her head to Carl Drew's wrist and bit as hard as she could.

'Aagh! You little devil,' Drew snarled between clenched teeth, but he held on to Emma's arm.

Wildly she swung the can of chemicals at him and the strong-smelling liquid sprayed out, splashing his arms and face. Carl Drew cried out and threw his hands up to protect his eyes.

Quickly Emma slipped from his grasp and ran. So desperate was she to reach the shelter of the trees that she almost ran into the Watchman.

'Come on, Watchman,' she gasped. 'Barrowby needs you now.'

At once a play of yellow fire began to flick across the grey stone man. It moved over the snakes so that they seemed to be alive. Then the Watchman's staff glowed yellow. It shone like a solid bar of light. Emma reached out to touch it. It came easily into her hand.

'James! Over here!' she called.

He appeared through the lich-gate, with Alistair Drew on his heels. As Emma held the staff, she noticed how different the hill looked. There were ridges in the field, almost as if a giant tail were wound around the hill. As if the hill were –

'– a dragon underneath the grass,' she cried. 'We are on the back of an enormous dragon.' It was just like in the carving.

'The very end of its tail is down there.' Emma stared at an odd arrow-shaped hump at the bottom of Church Meadow. 'And his head is –' She turned towards the wildwood behind the

church and as she did so a misty shape reared up from the trees. Two golden eyes as round as moons stared at them. 'James!'

Alistair Drew, caught in the gleam of the dragon's eyes, stopped dead. Then he turned and ran. Carl Drew, however, was walking slowly towards them. Even in the dim light, Emma could see dark angry patches on his skin where the chemical had splashed his face.

'You won't get away from me,' he growled at them. 'You can't do this to me and get away. I'll finish you!'

The storm was breaking now. A clap of thunder crashed above their heads. Drew looked up.

'How does a shepherd save his sheep?' Emma asked herself. 'He sets his dog on the wolves.' So slowly, but steadily, Emma pointed the shining yellow staff at Carl Drew.

Over the wood two yellow lights shone like moons – two huge yellow eyes stared at Carl Drew. Flashes of yellow fire filled the sky. The same yellow fire as the burning eyes.

Half-way down the hill Alistair Drew looked back. He saw Emma pointing the shining rod at

Carl and saw a huge shape looming in the sky above his brother.

'Run, Carl!' he yelled, but it was too late.

A long tongue of fire flicked from the sky and wound about Carl Drew. It seemed to hold him for a moment, to wrap him like shimmering barbed wire, then with a deafening crack it exploded all around him. The shock of it knocked him to the ground. His clothes smoked.

Alistair Drew stared in horror at his brother. He started to run back towards him, but a ball

of fire bobbed between them. He turned again and ran. The fireball followed him. Whenever he snatched a glance over his shoulder it was there, pushing him further down the hill towards Meadowfield Farm. When he was almost at the barn, it shot above him, cracking in the sky, burning yellow. Then it uncurled like a claw and stretched through the darkness until it touched the roof of the Drews' barn. On the hillside Alistair Drew stopped running.

'No! No!' he screamed as flames licked at the barn. 'The pesticide. It'll go up like a torch!'

As he spoke, the whole barn roared into black and orange fire. The pyramid of chemical drums burst and blazed and the force of the explosion threw Alistair Drew into the air and back on to the hillside.

As James and Emma watched the terrible blaze of the burning barn, it began to rain. And as the rain fell, the clouds thickened. The two golden lights above the hill winked shut.

'James,' Emma whispered. 'The staff.'

Together they watched as the bar of light faded and disappeared, leaving Emma's hand quite empty. Behind them, on the highest point of the hill, a pinprick of yellow light flickered, then went out. The statue of the Watchman stood as he always had, his stone stick with its stone snakes held firmly in his hand. While they stared at the statue they heard someone calling their names.

'James! Emma!' Matthew Waterwitch was hurrying towards them. 'What on earth . . . ?' He stepped forward and knelt by Carl Drew. 'He's still breathing. What happened?'

'I'm not sure,' said Emma. 'They had these cans. They were pouring stuff on the hill. Then the storm . . .'

'Lightning?' Matthew asked. 'Of course. It looks as if Carl has actually been struck. I think we'd better call an ambulance, don't you?'

Chapter Twelve

James and Emma were in disgrace. Creeping out of the house in the middle of the night had not gone down too well with Aunt Caro and Uncle Richard.

'It was my idea,' Emma tried to take the blame. 'My fault,' she said, but they wouldn't listen.

'Those Drew brothers were quite badly hurt by the electric storm,' Aunt Caro said. 'You can think yourselves very lucky that it isn't you in the hospital. You will stay in your rooms all day,' she went on in her sternest manner, 'and there will be no television for the rest of the week.'

They had spent most of the morning alone in their rooms, but when Matthew Waterwitch called to see them, Aunt Caro had to let them come down.

'Do you think Carl Drew really meant it, or

was he just trying to frighten us?' Emma asked as they walked downstairs.

'I don't think Alistair would have let him hurt us,' James replied. 'Still . . .'

'We'll never know, will we?' Emma finished off his thought. 'Should we tell?'

'I think we'd better,' James said. 'We'll start by telling Matthew.'

Matthew listened carefully to all they had to say.

'The Drews will be prosecuted,' he said. 'Those jerrycans are hard evidence and with all you've told me, the police will have a very strong case against the brothers Drew.'

'Are they still in hospital?'

'Carl has minor burns pretty well all over. He was lucky. A strike like that can kill a man. Do you know the lightning burnt the soles of his boots right off?'

'And Alistair?' James wanted to know.

'Concussion from his fall and a broken arm. He twisted when he fell. If you ask me they both got off very lightly.'

'Will Church Meadow be all right?' Emma wanted to know. 'Or did the Drews pour out enough of that stuff to kill it?'

'The Inspector was here first thing this morning. Fortunately, you interrupted the Drews before they'd had time to really poison the place. The plants will recover in time.'

'Then the meadow will become an SSSI?'

'Yes.'

'And Cruxton Housing will have to build its new estate somewhere else?'

'Yes,' said Matthew. 'They will.'

James and Emma came to the end of their week without television and Emma's holiday was nearly over. They only went back to Church Meadow once and they had to take Aunt Caro with them.

'That place has got you into trouble once too often,' she said. 'You're not going there alone.'

From the top of the slope they could see the whole of New Barrowby. Birds sang in the wood. A hedgehog snuffled in the ivy roots at the foot of the Watchman. Everything was absolutely normal.

'Did we really see a dragon?' James whispered to Emma as they stared down at the black ruin of the Drews' barn.

'Oh yes, James,' she said. 'We really did.'